Dedicated to the memory of Jan Ormerod

1946–2013

Little Hare Books
an imprint of
Hardie Grant Egmont
Ground Floor, Building 1, 658 Church Street
Richmond, Victoria 3121, Australia

www.littleharebooks.com

Text copyright © Jan Ormerod 2013
Illustrations copyright © Andrew Joyner 2013

First published 2013
First published in paperback 2013

Cataloguing-in-Publication details are available from the
National Library of Australia

978 1 742977 31 7 (pbk.)

Designed by Vida & Luke Kelly
Produced by Pica Digital, Singapore
Printed through Asia Pacific Offset
Printed in Shenzhen, Guangdong Province, China

5 4 3 2 1

*The illustrations in this book were created using brush and
ink drawings digitally coloured with ink wash and pencil.*

THE SWAP

by Jan Ormerod • pictures by Andrew Joyner

LITTLE HARE
www.littleharebooks.com

'Your baby brother is gorgeous,' said Mama Crocodile.
'He is as green as a grub, and his eyes are as yellow as egg yolks.'

Caroline Crocodile was jealous. 'He's smelly.'

'He loves to eat up
his fish and frogs,'
said Mama Crocodile.

Caroline was very jealous.
'He's no fun,' she said.

Mama Crocodile said, 'Look at his adorable snout.'

Caroline was very, very jealous.

'He dribbles.'

'He has such scaly skin and sharp little claws,' said Mama.

'He takes up all the room on your lap,' said Caroline.

But Mama Crocodile was busy giving baby brother a big, smacky-smoochy kiss.

Caroline was very, very, very jealous.

She wanted a big, smacky-smoochy kiss from Mama Crocodile.

Next day, Mama Crocodile said,
'This new hat is not exactly
what I want. I will go to the
Hat Shop and swap it for one
that is just right.'

'Be a good girl, Caroline,
and look after your
baby brother,' said Mama.
'I will be back soon.'

Caroline waited, and baby brother dribbled.

Then Caroline saw that they were outside the Baby Shop,
so she took him in.

'This baby brother is not exactly what I want,' she said. 'It's smelly and it dribbles, it's no fun, and it takes up all the room on my mama's lap. I want to swap it for one that is just right.'

'Of course,' said the assistant.
'How about a baby panda? So soft and cuddly.'

'Well, my mama does love yellow eyes,'
said Caroline.

'Why don't you try it and see?'

So, Caroline Crocodile took the baby panda to the cafe for a snack.

'Fish?' asked Caroline. 'Or frog?'

The baby panda ate the bamboo chair he was sitting on.
Then he ate Caroline's chair too.

Caroline took the panda back to the Baby Shop.

'No good,' said Caroline.
'Fussy eater.'

'How about this baby elephant with the adorable trunk?'
said the assistant.

'Well, the trunk looks like a snout, and my mama
loves a snout,' said Caroline.

Caroline Crocodile took the baby elephant to the fountain.

He trumpeted loudly and sprayed water over his back and onto passers-by. Then he sat on the edge of the fountain and it broke.

Caroline took the elephant back to the Baby Shop.

'No good,' she said.
'Too squirty.'

'Well, will you try twin baby tigers?'
said the assistant. 'Twice the fun!
And such sharp little claws.'

'My mama loves sharp claws,'
said Caroline.

The two teeny tigers took off to the Toy Shop.

They pushed the little ones off their chairs, scattered the jigsaw puzzles, knocked over the displays, ripped up the cuddly toys, crashed the cars and bit the books.

Caroline took the twin tigers
back to the Baby Shop.

'No good,' she said.
'Too tiring.'

'How about a baby giraffe?'
said the assistant.

'No good,' said Caroline.
'My mama likes scaly babies.'

'A baby pig?' the assistant suggested.

'No good,' said Caroline.
'My mama likes green babies.'

'Well, all I have left,' said the assistant,
'is this second-hand crocodile.
It is in lovely condition:
look at its shiny new tooth.'

'My baby brother, with a new tooth!
That is why he was dribbling!'
cried Caroline Crocodile.
'I'll have you back. You are still smelly
and dribbly, but you are not a fussy eater.
You are not too squirty or too tiring.

You are just right after all!'

Mama Crocodile came back with her new hat.

'What a good big sister you are to look after your baby brother so well,' she said. 'Why, he has a new tooth! When all his teeth grow he will be as beautiful as you are, Caroline, with your green scaly skin, your yellow eyes, your sharp little claws and adorable snout.'

And Mama Crocodile gave Caroline a big, smacky-smoochy kiss.